My Office Wife

The Friends to Lovers Series

by

Reba Bale

Table of Contents

Copyright

About This Book

Is someone still considered your "work wife" if you're both women?

Rachel and Brittany have been friends for a long time. Good friends. They both started at Phoenix Software on the same day and have worked on the same team ever since. For years they've joked around calling each other their office spouse, much to the consternation of the women they've dated.

But lately, things have felt different...

First, there's that time Brittany accidentally walks in on Rachel showering in the company gym. And there's that tiny little kiss after the office holiday party, the one neither of them can stop thinking of. And then there's an unexpected mix-up at the hotel on a company trip. When the two friends wind up sharing a room, they can't hide their feelings any longer.

It turns out that their feelings are more 'wifey' than friendly, but can their relationship survive the change?

"My Office Wife" is book eleven in the "Friends to Lovers" romantic novella series. Each book in the series is a steamy standalone featuring an LGBTQ couple making the leap from friends to lovers and looking for their "happily ever after".

Be sure to check out a free preview of Reba Bale's lesbian romance "The Divorcee's First Time" at the end of this book!

Dedication

This book is dedicated to everyone who's ever had an office spouse. It's a unique relationship, and one that makes your work life more enriching, even if it's always platonic.

Join My Newsletter

Want a free book? Join my newsletter and you'll receive a fun subscriber gift. I promise I will only email you when there are new releases or special sales, usually twice a month.

Visit my newsletter sign-up page at bit.ly/RebaBaleSapphic[2] to join today.

---

2.   https://bit.ly/RebaBaleSapphic

Brittany

Ten years ago...

"Welcome to Phoenix Software. My name is Madison Phoenix, and I'm thrilled to have you all join our team."

I gazed at Madison Phoenix with something akin to hero worship. One of the youngest female billionaires in the world, she'd started Phoenix Software in her college dorm room and quickly turned it into one of the most successful companies in the country. The company's first product was a social media scheduling and marketing system for businesses, but they'd expanded over the years to offer a variety of software solutions focused on small to medium sized businesses.

Phoenix was currently expanding to add an employee management system. The new program could handle timesheets, time off requests, and performance management functions. Industry insiders were predicting that it would blow programs like ADP and Workday out of the water.

With multiple preorders on the books already, a new team of customer support specialists was being stood up. The CSS team would work with companies one-on-one to create reports, troubleshoot issues, and help with implementation.

After five years of working at a rival payroll solutions company, I was ready to move into the big leagues. And Phoenix Software was the big leagues for sure.

I glanced around, noting that of the twelve new employees on the team there was only one man. One person appeared to be non-binary, and the rest of us were women. I wasn't surprised. Phoenix Software had a reputation for being a supportive working environment for people who were part of the LGBTQ community, probably because Madison herself was a lesbian.

And most of the senior managers too, or so I'd heard.

"Now I'd like to introduce you to Claire Langford. She will be your team lead, mentor, and taskmaster as we roll out Phoenix Employee Solutions. Good luck to all of you and again, welcome to the team."

As Madison strode out of the room I looked around again. A woman one row back kept catching my attention. She was stunning, with long, straight brown hair and deep brown eyes that darkened when she caught my gaze. I felt a little zing, then shoved it back down. There was no way I was going to ruin this incredible opportunity by having a workplace romance. No way. But maybe we could be friends.

Rachel

Last December...

"Are you ready to head to the party?"

Brittany startled, as usual super focused on her work. It was amazing how much this woman could tune out when she was concentrating. I couldn't reach that level of focus without headphones and a fresh dose of Adderall.

"Yeah, let me just save this document."

I sat on the corner of my desk and waited. We had been sharing an office now for over ten years, ever since we both came to work at Phoenix Software. Our very first day of work we'd been paired up as work partners, and we'd been inseparable ever since.

It was funny how well we got along, given that we were both very different. I'd been raised in a Jewish neighborhood in Brooklyn as part of a large, close family. I took the subway to school and went to synagogue every Friday.

Meanwhile Brittany was raised in the suburbs of Seattle in a family who only practiced their Lutheran religion on Christmas. Or at weddings and funerals. Her mother drove her to school every day and they had a big yard and a dog.

Brittany's mom had been a homemaker while my mom had always worked outside the home.

Where my family was nosy and noisy, hers was quiet and very much of the 'don't ask don't tell' variety. When Brittany had come out as a lesbian to her family they hadn't batted an eye, and they'd also not asked a single question. My family had been generally supportive when I came out, but they'd questioned me to death. Still did.

Brittany looked like the girl next door, with straight blonde hair, brown eyes, and a slim figure. She was gorgeous, and if we hadn't been such good friends, I would have totally been attracted to her.

When we first started working together, we'd mostly been work friends. We'd chat, have lunch, maybe go to a group happy hour. But gradually we'd started spending time together outside the office, much to the consternation of people we dated. Our coworkers joked around that we were each other's 'work wife' but the truth was, we were much more than that.

We started off as colleagues and gradually moved on to being friends. Good friends. The kind of friends who shared secrets and could finish each other's sentences.

"I'm ready."

Brittany stood up and stretched, the motion lifting her shirt enough to reveal a sliver of pale skin just above the waistline. My eyes fixed on the spot. I always teased her that she was a true Pacific Northwesterner, not a hint of melanin in her skin, unlike me.

We headed down to the restaurant on the next block that was hosting our company's annual holiday party. When we first started working at Phoenix Software we'd had these kinds of events in the cafeteria of our building, but as the company grew, we'd needed to seek out larger venues. Thanks to shrewd and creative leadership, the company was even more successful today than it had been when we started here years ago.

Brittany and I made our way around the party, talking and laughing with our coworkers. That was something pretty unique about Phoenix Software. Most people liked each other here. There wasn't that divide between management and staff like a lot of companies had, and there was very little inter-employee drama.

Even if Phoenix hadn't paid well, I'd stay for the great working environment and all the employee perks.

"Brittany. Rachel. Thanks for coming tonight."

Madison was the CEO of Phoenix Software, but she made it a point to learn everyone's names, especially her longer-term employees. I was amazed that she could keep us all straight.

"Thank you, Madison, it's a great party, as usual." Brittany responded, giving the CEO a bright smile.

"Have you two met my girlfriend, Camille?"

She tilted her head to the purple haired woman holding her hand. Camille looked to be a few years younger than Madison, and a little edgier with her purple hair and tattoos. But the way she and Madison looked at each other left no doubt that the two of them were deeply in love.

I realized that I recognized Camille.

"Don't you work at Morning Jolt?" I asked, referring to a coffee shop two blocks away from our office. They had great coffee and a nice assortment of pastries. Madison Phoenix had purchased the place a couple of years ago, although no one knew why.

Camille nodded. "Yeah, but I only do a shift or two a week there now," she explained. "I've been busy with my writing career."

"You're a writer?" Brittany asked, looking impressed.

Madison slid her arm around Camille's shoulders. "She's an excellent writer and starting to become quite popular too."

"What do you write?" I asked.

"Fantasy books with strong female protagonists."

"That's so cool. I'll have to look you up," I said. "I love to read."

Camille and Madison moved along, and we headed to the bar. Neither of us generally drank a lot, but tonight's signature cocktail was really hitting the spot. I couldn't say what was in it, but it was something chocolate and pepperminty that tasted delicious. And apparently stronger than I thought, because by the end of the night I was feeling decidedly tipsy.

"Oh my God, I think I'm drunk."

As usual, Brittany and I were on the same page.

"I have no idea how many of these I've had," I said, waving my empty glass around in front of me. "I don't think I've been drunk since I was in my early twenties."

"Same," she said.

Even though she was standing still, Brittany somehow stumbled a bit, one hand coming to brace herself on my shoulder. Our eyes met and held and for a minute I started having very inappropriate thoughts about my office wife. I searched her face, wondering what she was thinking, but everything seemed a little blurry. Oh yeah, probably because I was drunk.

"Should we grab an Uber and head home?" I asked, breaking the silence.

She pulled back with a shaky sigh. "Yeah."

Brittany and I lived two blocks apart from each other, so it was easy to share an Uber. After a quick stop at the restroom, we grabbed our coats and headed out front to wait for our ride.

It was a chilly night, with a light rain falling steadily, typical for Seattle in December. It had taken me a while to get used to the almost nonstop rain we got here for more than half the year, but I'd grown to love Seattle with its fresh air and greenery and slower pace of life.

A Toyota Corolla came screeching to a stop in front of us and Brittany and I slid into the back, greeting the driver. The back seat was small and cramped and as the driver took a corner on what felt like two wheels, the two of us slid into each other. Oops, guess we'd forgotten our seatbelts!

I widened my eyes at my friend dramatically and she laughed. Another turn brought us even closer together and I braced my hand on Brittany's thigh to keep from sprawling on top of her. As we'd been tossed around her skirt had hiked up, and my hand hit bare skin. I felt a little jolt.

Everything in me stilled, my gaze dropping to my hand. When I looked up again, Brittany was staring at my hand on her upper thigh, a contemplative look on her face. She licked her lips, and I couldn't help but feel aroused.

When she lifted her gaze, I had that weird feeling again. A feeling that definitely wasn't friendly.

The air between us seemed to heat up and before I knew what was happening, I moved forward. Brittany closed the remaining distance between us, her eyes bouncing between mine, and then our lips met. Her lips were so soft, and in the back of my mind I remembered her telling me about a new moisturizing lip gloss she'd discovered.

Brittany sighed, and I slid my tongue into her mouth, exploring. Her hands came to my head, holding me close, and her tongue tangled against mine. I slid my fingers under her skirt, caressing the silky skin of her thigh.

I tilted my head and deepened the kiss. I wasn't sure what was happening between us, but I liked it. My entire body was vibrating with excitement.

We both startled as the car came to a screeching halt, nearly tossing us against the front seat. We pulled apart, breathing heavily. I felt a sense of panic as I realized that I'd been kissing my best friend. What was I thinking? And why had she kissed me back?

"Here you go," the driver said, giving us a smirk that told me he'd been watching what was happening back here. "You girls have fun."

I scooted back, exiting the car as Brittany did the same. Her eyes looked wild and confused. I knew the feeling. The driver took off in a squeal of tires on pavement. Brittany turned around to look at me, the expanse of the sidewalk separating us.

"What was that?" she finally asked, her voice shaky. "What happened back there?"

"We're both drunk," I reminded her. "It was a fluke. We won't even remember this in the morning."

"Okay. Yeah. You're right." Brittany looked uncertain. "I'll um, I'll see you Monday."

She took off for the front door of her apartment, walking quickly.

"Yeah, okay," I called after her. "See you Monday."

As I walked the two blocks to my own apartment, I couldn't help but rehash what had just happened. In all the years that Brittany and I had been friends, I'd never once considered kissing her. I was confused why I had. That kiss had messed with me in a way that I never would have anticipated, if I'd ever anticipated kissing her, that is.

Damn those seasonal cocktails, they had totally messed with my mind.

You just forget all about it, I reminded myself sternly. *You and Brittany are too good of friends to mess this up.*

I just hoped I really could forget.

Brittany

Present day...

I walked into the locker room, intent on taking a shower. I wasn't actually planning to work out, I just wanted to freshen up before my date tonight. I didn't have enough time to go home, so I figured I'd pop down and shower before I left the office.

That was one of the great things about working at Phoenix Software. We had a cafeteria, a well-appointed gym that included a swimming pool, and free coffee, tea, soft drinks, and snacks available on every floor. They really took good care of us.

Tonight was my second date with a woman named Barb and I was pretty sure she was going to make a move on me. Honestly, even though I liked her a lot as a person, I wasn't super attracted to her. She was a little too butch for my tastes, but I figured that once we got started my body would get on board.

At least I hoped that was true. I'd been in a long dry spell, and I'd been horny as hell lately.

Of course, that probably had something to do with the thing that shall not be named. The Kiss. I always thought of it in capital letters like it was a movie title or something. It had been three months and still I couldn't get that damned kiss out of my mind.

It was probably because I hadn't kissed another woman since then, I reminded myself.

God, I hoped that was why. Because I needed to get rid of this inconvenient crush on my best friend. Our relationship was way too important to me to muddy the waters with an inconvenient crush.

I just needed to get Rachel out of that part of my mind, and I was hoping sleeping with this other woman Barb would be a nice reset for my brain.

The gym locker room was surprisingly quiet. It was always busiest in the mornings and during the lunch hour, but there were a few people who worked out after work.

Grabbing a towel, I headed towards one of the shower cubicles. The shower area was nice with individual changing rooms, high-end shampoo and soap, and dual level shower heads.

I opened the door to the closest shower cubicle and stopped short when I realized someone was in there. The door was ajar, and I hadn't heard any water running, so I thought the cubicle was empty. My eyes widened as I saw that it was Rachel inside.

She was totally naked, towel drying her long dark hair. Against my will, my eyes took a quick trip downward, cataloging perky breasts that turned upward as if her nipples were looking towards the sky, down to an indented waist, generously rounded hips, and thick but muscular thighs. My eyes fixed for longer than they should have on the patch of dark hair at her apex.

"Hey!" she said belatedly.

My eyes snapped back up to her face.

"Oh my God, I'm so sorry," I stammered. "The door wasn't closed all the way."

We'd changed clothes around each other before, but I'd always obeyed the unwritten rules of the locker room and kept my eyes to myself. Until now. Now I was going to have the image of her naked body burned onto my retinas.

"No problem," she said, her voice sounding unnaturally high.

Maybe it was my imagination, but I could swear that I saw her nipples hardening in my peripheral vision. Oh my God! Why was I still standing here?

I rushed out, grabbing my stuff from the locker and leaving the gym. It would feel too awkward to take a shower now. If Barb and I got intimate tonight, she'd just have to deal with me not being so fresh.

Three hours later I knew my freshness didn't matter. I wasn't going to be able to sleep with a woman I wasn't at least a little bit attracted to. Especially not after I'd gotten a view of Rachel in the shower.

Damn it, why had that happened? I didn't want things to be awkward between us now. And I knew instinctively that they would be. We could write off The Kiss as a drunken mistake. I didn't have the same excuse for staring at my office wife naked in the shower.

After a perfectly nice dinner with Barb, she kissed me. I pulled away and told her that I thought we were better off as friends. Fortunately, she didn't seem too offended about it.

Then I went home and did something I'd avoided doing for years: I pulled out my vibrator and got myself off while I fantasized about Rachel.

***

"Do you two have everything ready for your trip?"

I looked up as Claire entered the office. Several years ago, she'd been promoted from team lead to supervisor, and as two of the senior members of the team, we still worked very closely with her. I noticed that she looked a little frazzled.

"Are you okay, Claire?" I asked.

She shook her head, then nodded, her eyes cloudy. "Oh yeah, thanks. Everything is fine. I just have some personal drama going on with my ex-wife."

I was dying to ask for more details, but I knew Claire well enough to know she wouldn't like that. Professionalism was of the utmost importance to her. I'd worked with the woman for ten years and didn't even know she had an ex-wife.

"Well, I hope it all works out," I said sympathetically.

I had enough divorced friends to know that things were often super complicated, even when no kids were involved.

"Thanks. Do you need anything from me before you leave?"

Rachel and I were going to Las Vegas to help with a new customer who was about to launch our Employee Solutions program.

"Thanks, but I think we're good. It looks like the rollout will be pretty smooth. All of the pre-work went very well."

"Don't jinx us," Rachel joked.

She'd been pretty quiet around me the last three days since I'd walked in on her standing naked in the shower. We probably should talk about it, but I hadn't been able to bring myself to mention it. However, I'd had no trouble replaying the scene in my mind over and over again while I was alone in my bed, damn it.

"Where are you two staying?" our boss asked.

"Samson's."

At Claire's curious look I explained, "It's one of the older hotels and casinos, over in downtown Las Vegas. It's about a mile away from our customer's office and far enough from the Strip that it won't be so noisy and crowded."

I'd been to Vegas a few times and was not a fan of the Strip. I'd grown up around trees and open spaces and fresh air. Crowds, concrete, and cigarette smoke was not my idea of fun.

"Just don't get accidentally married," she teased.

I rolled my eyes. "This is business, not a romcom."

Rachel

"I'm sorry, but I'm only showing one room reserved, for a Miss Brittany White. I don't have any reservations for Rachel Rosenthal. The hotel is completely booked up due to conventions so I can't offer you another room."

Brittany's words from yesterday floated in my mind. Only one hotel room. Apparently, we were living in a romcom after all. Which was a problem, because ever since she'd accidentally walked in on me in the shower a couple of days ago, I couldn't stop thinking about kissing her. And more.

Well, if I was totally honest, I'd had those thoughts ever since we kissed in the back of the Uber right before Christmas. I'd just tried really hard to ignore them.

But in the locker room, I couldn't help but notice the way Brittany's eyes had explored my body. She'd liked what she saw, that much had been obvious. Her nipples had hardened, her pupils had blown wide, and when she'd checked out my pussy, she'd licked her lips. I don't even think she was aware of it.

Now all of the sudden I was painfully aware of the way she smelled, how soft her hair looked, and how fantastic her ass looked in the jeans she'd worn on the plane. With her blonde hair pulled up in a ponytail and her face completely free of make-up, she looked like the poster child for the All-American Good Girl Next Door. And I wanted to dirty her up.

Damn it! I needed to stop thinking about this. Brittany and I had been good friends and work partners for years. I didn't want to mess it up. Yet I also couldn't help but wonder how it would be if we got together.

"Please tell me the room you have available has two beds," Brittany gritted out, looking uncharacteristically annoyed.

Maybe she wasn't wondering about us getting together after all. Brittany was usually cheerful and sunny and positive, while I tended to be more serious and dour. She was the sunshine to my grumpy.

"Yes ma'am, the room has two double beds."

Brittany turned to me, summoning a smile that didn't quite reach her eyes.

"Well, it won't be the first time we've shared a hotel room."

It was true, we'd gone on a couple of short trips together, including one where she joined me for a weekend in San Francisco after my girlfriend at the time dumped me. Coincidentally, she dumped me because she was sure that something was going on with me and Brittany. At the time it had seemed completely out of the realm of possibility, but right now...well, let's just say that I was as glad as Brittany was that we didn't have to share a bed.

We dropped our stuff off in our room then headed out for dinner. We both refused drinks, clearly on the same page about staying sober around each other.

I couldn't help but notice that we were both quieter than normal at dinner. Where normally we'd be chattering throughout the meal, tonight there were periods of silence. They weren't uncomfortable silences per se, but they were definitely different.

After finishing dinner, we took a walk around the neighborhood, rolling our eyes at some of the crazy outfits and drunken stumbling we saw. We generally liked to scope out the area where we were staying when we went on a trip, both to get our bearings and also to get some exercise. But this time I was pretty sure that we were both prolonging our time away from the room on purpose.

When we finally got back to the hotel, we immediately got ready for bed. Brittany and I were both early risers, so we tended to go to bed early anyway. That's how we both ended up in bed by ten p.m.

I lay there staring at the ceiling, listening to Brittany's breathing. I could tell she was awake too. Finally, I couldn't take it anymore.

"Should we talk about what happened?" I asked.

"I don't know," she answered softly.

"We've always been able to talk about anything," I reminded her.

It was true too. We'd talked about books, politics, our crazy families, coming out, work frustrations, and the high points and challenges with every woman we dated. But ever since Christmas, things had been different between us, and now this shower thing had thrown us even more for a loop.

"I'm sorry I kissed you," I whispered. "At Christmas, I mean," I added unnecessarily. It wasn't like there had been another time.

"Why did you?" she asked.

I rolled over to stare at her in the dim light. She turned to face me as well, and I tried to see her expression, even though she was mostly a shadow in the darkness of the room. We hadn't pulled the blackout curtains, so even though we were a few miles away from the Strip, the lights of the city provided a bit of light through the sheer inner curtains.

"I don't know how it happened," I said. "We were sliding around in the seat with that stupid guy driving like a bat out of hell and I looked at you and you were so beautiful, and I was just drunk enough to think it was a good idea to kiss you."

I paused, and when she didn't respond, I asked, "Why did you kiss me back?"

"I've asked myself that question a hundred times. I could say it was because I was drunk, and that definitely was a factor, but it just, I don't know, it just felt right for some reason."

"It was a good kiss." My voice lifted at the end, making it a question.

Maybe it had been terrible. Maybe I'd just built it up in my mind based on some drunken memory.

"Yeah, it was."

After a long pause she continued, "I don't understand what's happening here, Rachel. We've always been good friends, never crossing any lines with each other. I mean, until Christmas I never even got a vibe between us."

I nodded, even though I wasn't sure if she could see me.

"But now after what happened, well, it's out there. Like an elephant in the room," I responded. "I can't stop thinking about it. But if something happens to mess up our friendship, not only will I lose one of my best friends, but it'll also mess up our work relationship too. I don't want that to happen."

She was right. I knew she was right. Still, her words hit me like a knife to the gut.

"Let's just try harder to forget about the kiss," I suggested. "You forget about seeing me naked. Let's just focus on work and trying to get things back to normal."

She sighed deeply.

"Agreed."

Brittany

"You want to input the number here."

Rachel and I were offering a hands-on training to help the managers at Bowman & Company learn how to use their new employee management software. But instead of focusing on my training duties, I was staring at the way Rachel's navy pencil skirt hugged the curves of her shapely ass.

It was like once I saw her naked, I couldn't help but think about how good she looked under her clothes. The irony was I hadn't even seen her ass that day. But that was okay, my imagination was filling in the details nicely.

I was thirty-five years old. A professional. A person who respected boundaries. And yet, if Rachel gave me any indication that it was okay, I would happily throw her down on one of these tables and lick her pussy until she came all over my face, audience be damned.

My panties felt a little damp just thinking about it.

When I was in college, we always joked about breaking the seal. It felt like you could drink beer for hours and be totally comfortable, but as soon as you went to the bathroom for the first time, you 'broke the seal' and after that, you had to pee every five minutes.

I'd broken the seal with Rachel, and now I just couldn't stop thinking about her. Even after we'd agreed last night to focus on keeping things platonic and to focus on our friendship, I still couldn't get my damned mind out of the gutter.

I didn't know what was wrong with me.

Through sheer will, I returned my focus back to work where it belonged. My job. We ended up staying pretty late at the Bowman & Company since we had to teach a session for the second shift as well.

By the time we left, we were too tired to find someplace to eat. Instead we took an Uber back to the hotel and ordered room service.

We sat side by side on the couch in our pajamas, eating crappy BLTs and watching a re-run of *Modern Family*. It was something we'd done a million times before, and yet, it felt different this time.

At some point Rachel slouched down with her feet on the coffee table, and when her head dropped against the back of the couch, I realized that she'd fallen asleep. That was one thing about Rachel – if she sat still for too long, she'd fall asleep no matter where she was.

I smiled and returned to watching television until I was ready to go to bed too. Then I roused her and walked her across the room to her bed, tucking her under the blanket. As she snuggled into her pillow I studied her face, relaxed in sleep. It was as familiar to me as my own.

I'd loved her as a friend for a long time, but I suddenly realized that somewhere along the way I'd also fallen *in love* with her. I gasped out loud in shock.

As I brushed my teeth, I wondered if this was why every relationship I had seemed to fizzle out. On some level, maybe I was comparing every woman I dated to Rachel and finding them lacking. Maybe all the women I'd dated who'd accused me of having feelings for Rachel had been more astute than I'd given them credit for.

One thing was for sure: I couldn't go on this way. As it turned out, I wouldn't.

***

The next day passed mostly like the first. We worked about ten hours with our clients, then after stopping at a local burger place for dinner, we headed back to our hotel room. It was our last night in town, and I was looking forward to being at home and in my own bed.

I was also looking forward to ending the unique torture of sleeping a few feet away from the woman who'd become a full-blown obsession for me since I'd seen her naked.

We walked into the hotel room, flipping on the entryway light, and I headed into the room to turn on the interior lights.

"Fuck!"

I swore as I tripped over a suitcase we'd pushed against the wall when we left this morning. My arms pinwheeled and Rachel came behind me, grabbing my waist and pulling me against her to keep me from falling.

"Thanks," I said breathlessly. "Nice reflexes."

Rachel's arms remained banded around my waist, her front pressed against my back. It felt completely natural to relax against her. I could feel her breath against my neck, and I could swear that I heard her subtly smell my hair.

My mouth turned dry, my heart rate speeding up as we stayed connected as if we were both frozen in place. I felt a trickle of sweat make its way down my spine, and the room suddenly felt uncomfortably warm.

"Rachel," I whispered.

My voice was full of need. I turned around in her arms, moving slowly, until we were face to face, staring at each other in the dim light. I saw her face change as she accepted the inevitable.

"We can't go on this way. Maybe we need to just get this out of our systems," I suggested.

One corner of her mouth lifted.

"We really are living out a romcom here, aren't we? Sharing a room, talking about banging away the sexual tension. But what happens if instead of getting it out of our systems we just wake the kraken?"

"I don't know, but we have to do something," I said. "The tension between us is too uncomfortable. Let's just promise each other that we'll have this night. One night only and nothing more. We'll just bang it out, whatever this is that's happening with us. Then tomorrow we'll go back to how we've always been, and never mention it again."

In the back of my mind, I had a bad feeling that this was a terrible idea, but my body was one hundred percent on-board.

"I promise."

I'd never heard Rachel sound so solemn. I reached up, cupping her cheeks with my palms, and stared into her eyes for a long moment.

Slowly I shifted forward, giving her time to pull back. Almost hoping that she would pull back because I didn't have it in me to be smart right now.

Instead, Rachel stayed perfectly still, her eyes soft, lips parted, waiting for me to close the distance.

So I did.

Rachel

Kissing Brittany again was a terrible idea. I knew this without a doubt. But I couldn't find it in myself to care right now, because the minute our lips touched, I felt a sense of inevitability. It was like everything we'd ever done had led up to this moment, and there was nothing we could do to change the course of our destiny.

Maybe some part of me had always known this was going to happen, because I didn't feel as surprised as I should have by how much I loved the feeling of Brittany's lips pressed against mine.

This time it wasn't a drunken impulse. We were completely sober, going into this wide-eyed, and as much as I worried that it might be a huge mistake, there was no way I could stop this now. I wanted her too badly.

Instead, I pressed the tip of my tongue against the seal of her mouth and when Brittany opened for me with a sigh, I swooped in. Our tongues tangled, exploring, and I kept my arms loosely around Brittany's waist. Meanwhile, her hands moved to my shoulders, holding me in place as if she thought I'd run away, and then eventually moving to wrap around the back of my neck.

I stepped closer, aligning my body against hers. I was three or four inches taller than her, and when I pressed my breasts against her torso, they slotted nicely just above her smaller breasts.

The kiss started off gentle, exploring, until suddenly the heat exploded between us. It was as if we had both been holding back and decided to let ourselves go at the same time. White hot heat flooded my body, and I lowered my hands to cup her ass, pulling her even closer so could grind my pelvis against her belly.

Brittany's hands moved up to tunnel into my long, dark hair. Pulling the strands lightly, she tilted my head to get a better angle, and deepened the kiss even more. I relaxed into it, losing myself into the sensation of her mouth on mine.

By the time we pulled apart, we were both panting for breath.

"Are we really doing this?" I asked.

God, I hoped we were doing this, but I felt like it was prudent for one of us to at least be the voice of reason. My best friend nodded slowly, thoughtfully. When I glanced down, the pulse in her neck was beating so hard I could see it.

"One time only, and then we never speak of this again, right?"

"Okay, yeah, sure," I agreed, even as I had a sinking feeling that one time would just make my hunger for her increase.

But if I could only have one time with her, I was damn well going to take it. We could deal with the consequences later.

I walked her backwards until we reached the closest bed. It was mine. Brittany always liked to have the bed closest to the window. One of a million little things I'd learned about her over the years.

She sat down on the edge of the bed, her feet on the floor, and I hiked up my skirt so that I could straddle her lap. Gripping her narrow shoulders, I kissed Brittany again, taking control. My kiss was rough and claiming.

But Brittany was not one to be passive. She slipped her hands between us and began unbuttoning my blouse, sliding it down my shoulders. I pulled back and shrugged it off before kissing her again. I could happily kiss this woman all night. She tasted like the burgers and chocolate shakes we'd had for dinner, and something that was uniquely her.

While we kissed, I reached behind me to unzip my skirt, and she shoved it higher until it was bunched around my waist. Brittany made a happy humming noise when she slipped her hand between my legs, discovering that the fabric of my panties was already wet with my arousal.

"You have too many clothes on," I told her.

She may have seen me naked already, but I'd never seen her in anything less than a swimsuit.

I slid off her lap and she stood up, making quick work of removing her business clothes. We both stood there in just our underwear, studying the other while we caught our breath. Suddenly, as if someone had fired a starter pistol or something, we flew back together, our bodies crashing against each other as we kissed again.

I'd never felt such intense passion before. If I'd been thinking clearly, it probably would have scared the crap out of me.

At some point we tumbled back onto the bed, hands reaching around each other to remove our bras, leaving us both only in our sodden panties. It didn't take long until those were gone too.

I shifted Brittany onto her back and lowered myself down her body until I could kiss her breasts. They were small – everything about Brittany was slim and petite – and I easily sucked most of the tissue into my mouth. I rubbed my tongue over the tip of one nipple while sucking everything I could fit into my mouth.

Brittany moaned, arching her back, her hands at the back of my head pulling me closer. She made a whining noise when I pulled away, then sighed as I shifted to suck her other breast into the moist heat of my mouth.

I shifted to the side just enough to slide my hand down her belly and over her mound. I was surprised to find her mostly bare, only a small patch of hair at her apex to meet my questing fingers. When I slipped a finger between her lower lips she cried out as if I'd electrocuted her or something.

She was dripping wet, and my fingers moved through her folds easily. I homed in on her clit, finding it already swollen. Without releasing her breast, I started circling her little bundle of nerves, moving close but never touching it.

"Rachel. Please."

I lifted my mouth off her breast to see her staring down at me with an expression on her face that could only be described as desperation.

"Do you want to come, baby?" I asked.

Her eyes widened at the endearment, but she didn't comment on it.

"Yes, it's...it's been so long. I really need to come."

"Okay then, don't worry," I reassured her. "I promise that I'll make you feel good."

I kissed my way down her belly, peppering little kisses on the outside of her pussy before finding her clit with my tongue. I tapped against it until her hips were rolling up against my face in a silent plea.

When I continued to tease her, she dug her fingers into my hair to hold me where she wanted me. I resisted. She was close, but if this was going to be the only time that we did this, I was determined to make her come her fucking brains out.

This needed to be the best orgasm of her life.

I pushed a finger into her channel, pumping in and out roughly. She was super tight, and for some reason I flashed back to the day she'd told me that she'd never slept with a man.

Unlike me, she had never been attracted to someone from the opposite sex. I'd slept with a few men when I was younger, mostly because I thought it was what I was supposed to do. Or maybe I was simply in denial about being a lesbian. Sex with men was okay, and I'd definitely enjoyed it, but it was nothing spectacular. I guessed I was technically a bisexual, but it had been years since I'd found a man attractive enough to consider dating him. Or doing anything else.

"Rachel! Please."

Brittany's breathless gasp brought my attention back to her. I peered up at her from beneath my eyelashes, then added a second finger into her channel and sucked her clit into my mouth. After that, it only took about thirty seconds before she stiffened, then started spasming beneath me, screeching my name.

Brittany

When Rachel sucked my clitoris into her mouth, I swear I saw stars.

I was thirty-six years old and had slept with my fair share of women over the twenty years since I'd officially come out. But this felt next level somehow. Maybe it was because Rachel and I already had a sense of intimacy from being such close friends for so many years.

But it felt like more than that.

I gripped the bedspread with my fingers, rolling my hips against Rachel's hand and mouth as I rode out the waves of my orgasm. It hit me hard, harder than I ever remembered happening before. My heart thundered in my chest and my vision turned fuzzy as wave after wave of pleasure rolled through my body.

I realized with a start that I loved Rachel – and not just as a friend.

That was why this felt so different. There had never been such strong emotions for me with anyone else I'd slept with. Being in love with my best friend and closest collaborator at work was a huge problem. So many things could go wrong. But right now, all I could do was focus on wringing every last ounce of pleasure out of this experience because we'd already agreed that it would never happen again.

Somewhere in the back of my mind I wondered if this night with Rachel was going to ruin me for other women.

I sagged against the bed, panting, and Rachel pulled her finger out of my channel, licking my cream off her fingers in a move that was so sensual I damn near came again just watching.

She moved up next to me, laying close but not touching me. I wondered if she felt as freaked out as I did. I turned on my side and threw my arm over her waist and my leg over hers.

"Just give me a few minutes to recover," I said, resting my head on her shoulder. "And I'll gladly reciprocate."

We snuggled like that for a few minutes until I caught my breath. I would have expected snuggling to feel weird, but somehow it felt totally natural.

"Your turn," I said, rolling off her.

I didn't want to leave her hanging for too long. If she was half as turned on as I was, she was dealing with some blue lady balls.

Rachel suddenly looked unsure.

"You don't have to. I'm fine."

"Oh my God," I said, cupping her pussy in my hand and giving it a little squeeze. "If you think I'm reciprocating out of obligation, you don't know me very well."

I remembered one woman who Rachel had dated about five years ago. It was the only time I'd ever heard her say she thought she might be in love. The two of them had been together for over a year, maybe eighteen months, and were talking about moving in with each other.

Mimi was a stunner, tall and thin with a body like a model. Rich and glamorous. I'd hated her on sight, not only because she seemed like a total bitch, but because of the subtle little ways she put Rachel down. It always felt like Rachel thought she was supposed to be pathetically grateful for Mimi's attention.

I'd tried to talk to her about it a few times, but she'd blown me off. They'd finally broken up and when Mimi dumped her. Rachel had been heartbroken, but I'd secretly thought it was for the best.

I learned later that she frequently told my friend that it had always been a chore to go down on her. Rachel took 'too long' to come, and was a little too 'pudgy', according to Mimi. When Rachel tearfully told me all this after they'd broken up, I remembered being completely enraged. It had taken everything in me not to drive over to that snobby bitch's house and punch her in the face.

Hearing Rachel act like me getting her off was going to be a chore broke my heart.

I shifted again until I was laying on top of her, my elbows on the outside of her shoulders, surrounding her. I shoved one thigh between her legs and as I kissed her, I ground my thigh against her pussy.

When she was writhing beneath me, I rolled off her again, laying on my back next to her. My thigh felt damp from her arousal.

"Hop on," I said, pointing at my face. "I want to smother in your juices."

Her eyes widened.

"Holy crap, no one's ever made me almost come just by talking before."

"I've got a lot of tricks in my arsenal," I said smugly. "Now give me a taste."

Rachel straddled my head, gripping the top of the headboard as she lowered herself over my face. I grabbed her hips, pulling her down more as I inhaled the scent of her arousal.

Tilting my head, I kissed at the juncture of her thigh, across her mound, and down to the other thigh, stopping to suck her skin into my mouth. She gasped as I marked her, her thigh muscles relaxing so that she was more fully sitting on my face.

I delved right into her pussy, burrowing my tongue and my nose between her folds. My tongue moved up and down, exploring her until my mouth was flooded with her taste.

For someone who'd told me that it took her a long time to come, she seemed pretty close already. She was dripping wet as she ground against my face. I couldn't help but feel a sense of feminine satisfaction at how responsive she was to me.

I circled my tongue around her opening before finally dipping in, then pulling back. She made a tiny little whining noise, and I did it again and again until she finally gasped, "Brittany! You're killing me."

With a chuckle, I shoved my tongue as deep as it could go, then reached my hands up to pinch her nipples, one in each hand. While I played with her full breasts, I fucked her with my tongue, gratified when she relaxed enough to meet me with each stroke.

When I glanced up, Rachel's head was thrown back, eyes closed, face the very picture of ecstasy as she rode my face. I felt her inner muscles flutter around my tongue and then she was coming, her juices spilling over my tongue as she cried out my name.

I released her nipples and used my hands on her hips to control her motions and prolong her orgasm. When she finally sagged forward, totally spent, I slid out from underneath her. She collapsed on the bed, and I pulled the blankets up before snuggling into her side. Reaching over, I turned off the lamp and fell into a deep, dreamless sleep.

Rachel

When I got up in the middle of the night to use the bathroom, I found Brittany spread out next to me like a starfish. Her arms were opened wide, one of them shoved under my head like a pillow, and her short legs were spread just as wide. Seeing her sleep with such abandon cracked me up.

After I used the facilities, I hunted around for my phone, plugging it into the charger and setting the alarm so we wouldn't miss our exit meeting at Bowman & Company.

The rollout had gone well, and Brittany and I had completed the entire project ahead of schedule, which meant we'd both be receiving a nice bonus from Madison Phoenix. The owner of the company offered generous incentives for exceeding expectations, and it motivated us all to work towards excellence.

I flashed back to my first day of work at Phoenix. I'd noticed Brittany right away, admiring her white blonde hair, pale skin, and expressive eyes. I'd been drawn to her, although it hadn't felt romantic. It had been more like she was the sun, and I was pulled into her orbit. I was new to Seattle at the time, and I immediately wanted to be friends with her.

When we were assigned to the same team and given an office to share, I'd been thrilled. Despite our different backgrounds and personalities, Brittany and I had become fast friends as well as close collaborators at work. She helped bring some fun and levity to my serious personality, and I helped ground her. People at work called us the 'power duo' because we always brought our projects in on time and on budget.

Over the years we'd had the opportunity to get our own offices and work with other teams but had chosen to stay in place so we could bounce ideas off of each other and remain work partners. No sense messing with success.

When we'd first become friends, some of our coworkers had assumed that we were dating, despite our denials. After they'd met a few of the people we dated, they'd started calling us each other's 'office wife'.

I'd never heard that phrase, but thanks to a Google search I'd learned that people were calling us that because we spent so much time together and were connected like a married couple, but without the romantic element to our relationship.

I just hoped that Brittany and I hadn't just ruined a good thing by sleeping together. It felt so right to be in her arms, but when morning came, we needed to go back to the way things were. It was what we'd agreed to.

But as I climbed back in bed and snuggled close to Brittany, I had a bad feeling that going back to normal would be harder than either of us was expecting.

When I woke up again, Brittany was awake and dressed, sipping a cup of coffee while looking at her tablet. She was probably checking Instagram. She'd been obsessed with that app since the first time she'd heard about it. Personally, I had no interest in any of the social media platforms.

"Good morning," I said, my voice scratchy.

She gave me a brief smile over her tablet but avoided my gaze.

"Good morning. I made some crappy hotel coffee to get us by until we could get something better."

"Thanks. I can't believe I didn't hear you get up."

I usually was a light sleeper, but laying next to Brittany, I'd slept like the dead.

As I sat up in bed, I realized I was still naked from the night before. Suddenly self-conscious, I wrapped myself up in a sheet, grabbed my suitcase, and headed into the bathroom to shower and get ready for the day. When I emerged a little while later, Brittany had switched to her laptop.

"Madison is thrilled about our work here," she told me. "She sent us and Claire an email saying that the CEO at Bowman & Company personally called her to say how thrilled he was with our work."

"Oh wow, that's awesome. I'm seeing a nice bonus in our future," I said with a smile. It was always nice when a project went well. It was good for the company, and for our bank accounts too.

"Definitely. I'm already making a mental list of things I want to buy."

Brittany closed her laptop, and we packed up our stuff so we could head over to our meeting at Bowman & Company.

Just like we'd agreed to last night, we went through the day deliberately acting normal, pretending as if nothing had happened between us. In a way I was glad we were keeping to our agreement. Honestly, I needed more time to process my feelings. And I did have feelings, which was a huge problem.

So I followed Brittany's lead, acting like I hadn't tasted her pussy or come all over her face, even as my feelings were the tiniest bit hurt that she seemed completely unaffected by what happened last night. I mean, I knew her pretty well, and I wasn't even seeing a glimmer of acknowledgement of what had happened.

I admired her ability to segregate her emotions even though it made me feel like shit.

We spent the morning wrapping things up at Bowman & Company, then headed to the airport for our flight back to Seattle. By the time we landed at SeaTac Airport it was after five, so we grabbed an Uber back to our neighborhood. The driver dropped me off first, and like I'd done a million times, I waved goodbye and promised to see Brittany at work the next day.

But as I entered my cold, empty apartment, I couldn't help but relive the night we'd spent together. I had a tendency to overthink, and it was in full force tonight as I analyzed every minute of my trip with Brittany.

Even though I reminded myself that we'd promised to have a one and done, I was finding it hard to pretend like our relationship hadn't fundamentally changed last night. I wondered why it was so easy for her to go back to normal and pretend like nothing had happened, while I'd struggled all day to avoid doing something stupid like pulling her into my arms. Or professing my newly discovered romantic feelings for her.

I desperately needed to talk to someone about what was happening between us. The problem was, Brittany was usually the one who I talked to in times like this. I had other friends of course, but not anyone I could talk to about something this huge. I paced around my apartment, talking to myself and sorting through my feelings and going around and around until I felt like I was going crazy.

Finally I dug out the business card for a therapist I'd seen after my break-up with Mimi. My therapist Monica had really helped me with processing my emotions around our break-up and had even helped me to finally acknowledge all the ways that Mimi had been emotionally abusive.

If anyone could help me figure this out, it would be my therapist.

Brittany

The next day was Friday and I'd never been so glad to see the end of the week in my life. I hadn't slept a wink last night, my mind swirling nonstop as I relived that last night in Las Vegas with Rachel. I know we'd promised each other that we'd go back to normal after our night together, but it was way harder than I'd anticipated.

I kept finding myself studying Rachel, trying to determine what she was thinking, but for the first time in our friendship, she was keeping her feelings close to the vest. Maybe that meant it hadn't been as fun for her as it was for me? Was I the only one dealing with these complicated emotions?

When I got to the office I put in my headphones, turning up the music as I tried to concentrate on my job. Still, I was aware of where Rachel was at every moment. It was frustrating, but I told myself that if I was patient, these feelings would pass, and Rachel and I could go back to just being friends.

That night I went out for dinner with my friend Colleen. We'd met at a lesbian speed dating event years ago and even though we hadn't clicked as romantic partners, we'd become good friends.

I met her at Miller's, a dive bar in her neighborhood that was charmingly unpretentious. Seattle had a lot of frou-frou places and while those had their place, sometimes it was nice just to have a beer and some salty French fries in a place that wouldn't dream of serving kale or artisanal cheese.

We greeted the owner, Big Bob, who gave us both a hug before pointing at an empty booth. When the waitress came over, we ordered beers, burgers, and fries.

"How's Mia?" I asked my friend.

Colleen and Mia had been high school rivals who'd run into each other a couple of years ago on Valentine's Day. Mia had been in the middle of being publicly dumped and Colleen had taken her out for a drink, right here at Miller's. The two former enemies became friends, then they fell in love. The two women had been together ever since. They were a great couple and I liked Mia quite a bit.

"She's doing okay," Colleen answered. "She's baking cookies tonight."

"It's not Christmas," I teased.

Colleen and Mia were famous in our group of friends for their elaborate and incredibly tasty Christmas cookies. They'd given me so many cookies last year I'd had to bring some of them into the office to share with my coworkers to keep myself from eating them nonstop.

"Mia has been volunteering at a senior center, so she thought she'd bring them a treat," Collen explained.

"Gosh, that's sweet."

My friend's expression turned soft. "Yeah, she's pretty great."

I felt a twinge of sadness that I didn't have what Colleen and Mia had. That easy camaraderie and unconditional love was something I'd longed for my entire adult life. There was only one person I could see myself having that kind of relationship with, but Rachel and I had committed to remaining only friends. I needed to honor that.

"What's up with you?" Colleen asked, tilting her head to study me. "You seem different somehow. Kind of...dull, almost."

"Are you calling me boring?" I laughed.

"No, I mean dull like not shiny. You're usually so full of life, but tonight you're subdued. Kind of sad. What's wrong? Is something bothering you?"

"Can I tell you something in confidence?" I leaned forward in the booth, even though I hadn't seen anyone I knew in here.

Colleen leaned forward in response.

"Of course. What's going on?"

I spent the next hour pouring out the story, starting with the unexpected kiss at Christmas.

"You two are the only people who would be surprised by that kiss," Colleen interjected. "Everyone who has spent any time with the two of you thinks you've been secretly pining for each other."

I rolled my eyes. "Pining? This isn't a Victorian romance novel."

"You know what I mean. Now what happened after the kiss?"

I continued with the story, including seeing Rachel naked in the shower and our decision to sleep together while we were in Las Vegas.

"Well, how was it?" she asked. "I'm assuming good since you're all twisted up about it."

I nodded and felt a flush rise up my pale cheeks.

"It was the best sex of my life. There was nothing awkward about it, you know? Everything was in sync." I sighed deeply, then added, "But we agreed to only doing it one time to try to get it out of our system."

Colleen snorted but didn't comment as I continued.

"I know it's the right thing to do, to follow our agreement and pretend like nothing ever happened, but I'm finding it really hard to do."

"Why is it the right thing to do?" Colleen asked. "You're both single. If there's something between you, why not explore it?"

I flopped back against my seat.

"I don't want to lose Rachel as a friend."

"What if you can be more? Friends and lovers?" she asked. "You wouldn't be the first couple to start off as friends before getting together romantically. I know several couples who went that route and found their mythical happily ever after with a close friend."

I shook my head. "I can't take the chance that things won't work out and I'll lose not only a close friend, but also my office wife and closest collaborator."

"Well, then you're just going to have to date someone else. That's the best way to get someone out of your mind."

Everything in me recoiled at Colleen's suggestion.

"Maybe you should talk to Alice, remember how she did that ten date challenge when her sister came out as a lesbian? She had women lining up to go on a date with Rebecca. Alice will fix you up with someone new for sure."

I set my chin on my hand and sighed. "I don't want to go on a date with anyone who isn't Rachel, but unfortunately she seems completely unaffected by our night together."

"Sounds like you have a big problem then. Because either you've caught feelings and she hasn't, or you both have feelings and you're both too chicken shit to take a chance and admit it."

I took a long swig of my beer as Colleen continued.

"Maybe the problem is that Rachel is better at compartmentalizing her feelings than you are," she said thoughtfully. "She's always pretty unruffled, where you are more likely to wear your heart on your sleeve."

"Well I can't wear my heart on my sleeve now, because Rachel will see it and then things will be awkward if she doesn't feel the same."

"I still don't think it would be a bad thing for you to talk to her about how this affected you, Brittany. You two can talk about everything. I don't understand why this is different. The worst-case scenario is you tell her you like her romantically and she says she doesn't feel the same. At least you'd know where you stand then."

"Yeah, you're right," I told my old friend. "I know you are. But I don't think I'm ready to put myself out there like that. There's too much at stake."

Rachel

Three weeks later...

"How's it going with you and Brittany? Have you resolved things yet?"

I sighed and slid farther down in my chair. As usual, my therapist looked completely unfazed even while her eyes studied me like a bug under a microscope.

Monica was in her late fifties with steel gray hair. She wore a broomstick skirt and half a dozen crystals. Her appearance screamed 'hippie grandma' but I knew better than to let that fool me. The woman was empathetic and kind, but she was also hard as nails and didn't miss a damned thing.

"It's been three weeks since we slept together. And on the surface, things are fine," I said. "We're working on projects together, going to our weekly yoga class, occasionally texting each other. But there's, I don't know, like a forced casualness to it. Like there's nothing deep."

Monica studied me for a long moment.

"What I hear you saying is that adding sexual intimacy to your relationship impacted the natural intimacy you already shared as close friends."

"Yeah." I sighed deep enough that I saw my hair lift away from my face.

"And how does that make you feel?"

I hated this question intensely every time Monica posed it. But I'd been seeing her long enough to know she'd keep badgering me in that calm way of hers until I broke and answered the question anyway.

"I feel...sad. I miss my best friend, you know? Every time we're close, I want to grab her and kiss her. She's clearly moving on, putting what happened behind us just as we agreed. But we're not back to normal. In fact, we're nowhere near normal. I heard Brittany telling someone in the office that she has a blind date tonight. That's the kind of thing she used to share with me."

"You miss your friend."

I nodded.

"Maybe you should tell her that. It's likely she's feeling the same way."

Monica was probably right. Brittany and I shared almost everything with each other, and we had such an easy rapport that anyone who was around us for any length of time commented on it. It's why everyone called us office wives.

No matter how Brittany felt about what happened between us in Las Vegas, she had to be missing the ease of our old relationship. I was sure of it.

"I just...I had a bad feeling sleeping together would mess up our relationship, and clearly it did." I rubbed the heels of my hands over my eyes. "On the one hand, I wouldn't trade that night for anything. But on the other hand, I wish it had never happened, not knowing what I know now."

"Intimacy changes things, that's natural. But you both knew that going in, correct? You even discussed it beforehand," Monica reminded me.

"That's right, we did. I guess we both thought we'd be able to put what happened in a little box, shut the lid, and go on with our lives as if nothing ever happened. But we were wrong."

"Does Brittany moving on make you want to try dating again?"

I shuddered in revulsion. "God no."

"Do you think it's possible that Brittany is going on a blind date because she thinks that's what you want?" my therapist asked.

I frowned. "What do you mean?"

"You've always told her that after your relationship with, um..." she peered down at her pad of paper.

"Mimi?"

"Yes, that's right, Mimi. Since the breakup with Mimi, you've been very clear that you don't want a serious romantic relationship. You've told me this. You've told her that."

When I nodded, she continued, "It may be she's having the same desires as you to explore a deeper personal relationship, but if you're both pretending like it never happened.... well, maybe she's just respecting your wishes and doing her best to move on like you originally agreed to do."

"Do you really think so?" I asked, feeling hopeful for the first time in weeks.

"Honestly, I have no idea, Rachel."

She gave me a look I couldn't interpret.

"There's only one way to find out. Take a risk. Your friendship has already been impacted anyway. Maybe it's time to talk to your best friend about your feelings. Honestly."

I stewed over Monica's words all night, in between wondering about how Brittany's date was going. Were they laughing? Kissing? Maybe more? Brittany wasn't one to have sex on the first date, but maybe she'd made an exception this time. The curiosity was killing me.

By the following morning I couldn't take it anymore. Being in this limbo state where I didn't know what was going on was too hard. Monica was right. One of us needed to open up and take a chance. I guess it was going to be me.

I threw on some clothes and walked the few blocks over to Brittany's place. I let myself into the building with my key – we were at each other's places so often we'd exchanged keys years ago—then ran up the stairs up to her floor. Taking a deep breath, I knocked.

When the door opened, Brittany looked at me in surprise. It was early Saturday morning and she was still wearing her pajamas. I usually slept in my sweats or just a long tee shirt, but my friend had a penchant for whimsical pajamas. Today's were pink with huge red cartoon hearts on them. With her long blonde hair tangled around her face, she looked young and adorable.

"Oh hey. Did we have plans that I forgot about?" she asked.

I shook my head. "I was hoping we could go for coffee and talk about what happened in Vegas."

My eyes widened as I remembered that she'd had a date the night before. "I mean, if you're alone."

She gave me a strange look as she pulled the door open. "Of course I'm alone. Let me get dressed and then we can go."

I hung out on the couch until she returned wearing jeans and a sweatshirt. She'd pulled her blonde hair back in a headband, something she liked to do on the weekends to keep it out of her face. Brittany's hair was fine and prone to breaking, so she tried not to pull it up too often lest she break some off.

It was funny, after so many years as close friends, I knew the most minute details about my friend. Except how she was feeling about me.

We walked in silence down the street to a coffee shop we often frequented, picking up coffee and bagels. When we settled at the table, Brittany looked at me expectantly, though her eyes looked troubled.

"I hate the way things are between us now," I blurted out. "Sleeping with each other ruined everything."

Brittany

I wasn't really surprised when Rachel showed up at my door. It had been three weeks since we'd had sex together, and instead of moving past it, we'd been growing apart, exactly what we'd both feared would happen.

The difference was that my solution was to pull away more and stick my head in the sand, where Rachel tended to confront things directly. I loved that about her. She was right, we needed to talk. The last few weeks we'd been acting like casual friends instead of two people whose lives had been intertwined for years. I hated it. I missed my friend.

I also loved her. Loved her as a woman, not just a friend. As much as I'd argued with myself about that point over the last few weeks, it was an inescapable fact. But for once in our friendship, I hadn't known how Rachel felt, and so I'd assumed the answer was 'nothing'.

I should have known better. I should have known she was feeling our distance as acutely as I was.

"I hate it too," I replied softly. "I miss us, Rachel. Things were always so easy between us and now, well I don't really know where we stand. We made a big mistake sleeping together."

She studied me carefully.

"Did we?"

My heart started to thump. Was she implying what I thought she was?

"Didn't we?"

Rachel rolled her eyes.

"Look, one of us has to be brave here, so I guess it's going to be me. I don't regret sleeping with you at all."

I reared back in shock. "You don't?"

"No, the only thing I regret is that we agreed to only do it once."

My heart was pounding so hard I was feeling a bit dizzy. Was she saying what I thought she was saying?

"But our friendship...," I protested.

"Can change and grow if we want to be together romantically. And the fact is, I want that. To be together romantically, I mean. And I'm hoping you do too."

I searched her face. She looked so earnest and hopeful that I wanted to cry.

"I'm just...I don't understand how this happened." I said. "I mean, for years we were good friends, then we have one drunken kiss, well and there's the time I saw you naked in the shower, and ever since then, I can't stop fantasizing about you."

"Isn't this how it happens in all your romcoms?" she teased.

My love of stupid romcoms was legendary. I watched every holiday romance I could, especially those Christmas ones on the Hallmark Channel. Rachel always pretended to hate them, yet she watched them with me every year. That was the thing about my friend, she acted crusty on the outside, but she was soft and gooey on the inside.

"One day the girl takes off her glasses," Rachel continued, "or she falls off a ladder into her best friend's arms, or they share a kiss to make a fake relationship look real, and boom! It's like they see each other in a different way, and all the sudden they're in love."

"Love?" The word came out like a high squeak.

Rachel leaned forward. "I've loved you as a friend for a long time, Brittany. But now I love you as a woman too."

When I just stared at her in shock, she deflated a little bit. I saw her smooth her expression into a neutral mask.

"It's okay if you don't feel the same, honestly. I just wanted to tell you how I feel. We've always been open with each other."

I shook my head, clearing my racing brain. She started to push back her chair, like she was trying to leave. I reached out my hand and grabbed her wrist, stalling her progress. Her eyes shot to mine.

"I love you too, Rachel."

"You do?"

"Yeah, I really do."

Then we just smiled at each other for a full minute, probably looking like a couple of loons to anyone who walked by.

"What happens now?" Rachel finally asked.

"Well, I think we need to get to know each other as romantic partners."

"So, you're saying we should date?" she clarified.

"Yeah, that's probably a good way to start," I said. "I mean, I know we know each other well as friends, but we could go on dates and get to know each other as potential partners."

"Oh, because I had a different idea," Rachel said, giving me a mischievous look.

"What's that?" I asked.

"We go back to your place and pledge not to leave the bed until we've both come at least a dozen times. We won't stop fucking like bunnies until we've had our fill of each other."

My panties damn near incinerated at the image that created in my mind. Rachel's eyes darkened, letting me know she knew the effect she was having on me.

"What if we never get our fill of each other?" I asked curiously.

"Well, then we'd better stock up on food and water," she said. "Because we're going to need to keep our energy up."

I stood up and held my hand out to her, gratified when she wrapped her fingers in mine.

"Let's go."

Rachel

Brittany and I race-walked back to her apartment, our fingers tightly wrapped together, and I felt a sense of relief. Three weeks was too long to be apart, even if it had been emotional distance. Sitting across from her in that office, unable to talk about my day, it had been torture.

We climbed the stairs, and as soon as we got through the front door, Brittany pushed me against the wall, grabbing my head to pull me down for a kiss. I went willingly, opening for her questing tongue.

It felt like her hands were everywhere: on my back, cupping my ass, sliding down the zipper of my jeans. Meanwhile I stroked her back, content to keep her close.

At least until her little hand slid underneath the waistband of my panties. My entire body jolted as she cupped my pussy, giving it a firm squeeze before sliding a finger inside my channel. I was already wet, and her finger moved in and out easily.

"Oh my God," I gasped.

When she added a second finger, I wrapped one leg around her legs, changing the angle. I rolled my hips against her hand, my back arching against the wall, biting my lip.

I knew I should be reciprocating, doing something other than standing there moaning, but I was completely overcome with sensations. It took all my concentration to remain standing as I fucked myself against her fingers. It was like my entire body was short-circuiting right now, my brain shutting down as I focused only on the heat filling my body.

"Take off your shirt," she ordered.

I loved this bossy side of her and hastened to comply.

"Now your bra."

The entire time she continued stroking me with those talented fingers. I reached behind me, trying and failing a couple of times before I remembered how to unlatch my bra. When I'd freed my breasts, Brittany immediately lowered her head and latched onto one of my nipples. I made a squeaking noise as she drew deeply, the sensation zinging all the way down to my already overheated core.

I'd always struggled to disconnect my brain during sex. Even in the most enjoyable scenarios, I was still in my head to some extent. Because of that, I could never completely let go. Several women I'd been with had been frustrated by how long it took me to orgasm, if I did at all. But somehow, Brittany knew exactly what to do to extract the maximum amount of pleasure from my body.

She pulled off my breast long enough to order, "Come for me, Rachel."

Then she sucked my other nipple into her mouth and bit down hard. I moaned loudly, and then I was coming faster and harder than I had in my life.

"Brittany! Oh my God."

It was all I could get out before I completely lost the power of speech. My entire body shook with the force of my orgasm, and when my standing leg started to give out, Brittany shoved her thigh between my legs, supporting my weight and keeping me upright as I rode out the waves of intense pleasure.

When I finally sagged against the wall, totally spent, she removed her fingers and brought them to my mouth. Obediently I opened up and cleaned my essence off her skin. It was erotic as hell.

"I, um, oh wow. I need to sit down," I said, sliding to the floor.

It was only when I slid to the floor that I realized I still had my jeans and panties wrapped around one ankle.

Brittany sat across from me, legs crossed, a sunny smile on her face. God, I loved that smile.

"That was fun," she said smugly.

"Fun? I'm pretty sure I went blind there for a minute."

"I had no idea you'd look so beautiful when you come," she mused. "I mean, not that I thought about it a lot, but if I had, I guess I would have pictured you looking all intense and growly, the way you do when we play pickleball. But instead, you look soft. Dreamy. Sweet. It's so fucking adorable."

I surged forward, pushing her onto her back and draping myself on top of her.

"Adorable?" I asked. "I'm too old to be adorable."

Brittany reached up and stroked my cheek. "You're perfect just the way you are, Rachel. You don't need to be any different."

I knew she was giving me a deeper message. Letting me know that she wasn't going to be like Mimi and expect me to change to earn her love. And I appreciated that, because even though I'd done a lot of work on myself since that relationship, there still was a tiny part of me that wondered if I was good enough.

Brittany pulled me down for a quick kiss.

"How about you eat my pussy in the bedroom?" she asked. "This floor is way too hard for fucking."

"Well, aren't you a romantic?" I teased.

"You love me anyway though, right? You haven't changed your mind or anything?"

"Not a chance," I vowed. "I love you and I'm in love with you, Brittany."

"Good, then we're on the same page. Now let's go get naked."

Brittany

When we got to the bedroom, we ended up snuggling for a while. It was fine. I could see that Rachel was wrecked from the intensity of her orgasm, so I encouraged her to move in close and take a little snooze.

"I promise I'll get you off in a few minutes," she said sleepily.

I stroked her hair.

"Didn't you sleep last night?"

"I haven't slept since the night we were together. One night with you and I lost the ability to sleep alone."

As she dozed next to me, I whispered, "You'll never have to sleep alone again, love."

When she woke up later, she made me come so many times I forgot my name. And that's how we spent the rest of the weekend. Just like we'd fallen into an effortless friendship, we slipped easily into the role of girlfriends.

On Monday we requested a meeting with our boss, Claire. While Phoenix Software didn't have a policy against coworkers at the same level dating since there wasn't a power dynamic in play, we both felt that it was only professional to let our boss know about the change in our relationship status.

Claire looked frazzled when we got to her office for our appointment. Claire never looked frazzled. Rachel and I exchanged a look.

"How are you doing, Claire?" Rachel asked carefully. "Is everything okay?"

Claire sighed deeply. "Oh yeah, I've just got some personal things going on. But that's neither here nor there. How can I help you two?"

"We'd like to report that we are in a romantic relationship," Rachel said formally. "For the record."

Claire frowned, looking between us.

"I thought you two were in a relationship already?"

"No, we've been good friends, but lately things have...um, changed between us and..."

When Rachel continued to hem and haw I blurted out, "We're dating now. Officially."

Claire leaned back in her chair with a smile.

"Well, first of all you don't have to tell me that, since neither of you is supervising the other. However, if you think your personal relationship will get in the way of your work, we can transfer one of you to another team."

"No." We spoke in unison.

"I can't believe you two weren't already dating," she said, her tone almost bemused. "I mean, I've thought for years that there was more there than just an office wife situation."

She stood up, signaling that the meeting was over. "Well, thank you both for coming. I'll be sure to document that you informed me of this change."

We stood up and started to leave.

"Oh, and one more thing, since this is new, please remember to conduct yourselves professionally while you're in the office. If I see ass prints on the conference table or hear moaning coming out of the restroom, I'm going to be pissed."

"Got it," we said in unison.

Rachel and I walked side by side to our office, and I closed the door behind us. The wall was made out of glass, but closing the door would give us a modicum of privacy.

"That was anticlimactic," I said. "I somehow thought that would be like a whole thing."

Rachel looked a little shellshocked.

"Yeah. But I'm confused. Why did people think we were seeing other people if we were secretly dating?"

"Who knows?" I asked. "Maybe they thought we had an open relationship? The important thing is, we don't have to hide our relationship."

Rachel shook her head. "No, the important thing is that we don't have to hide our feelings."

I sat at my desk and met her gaze across the small office. "Yeah?"

"Yeah. Like the feeling that I want to spend every day for the rest of my life making you happy."

"You do, huh?" I asked teasingly.

"I do."

"We should probably agree to some rules," I said. "Even if everyone knows we're dating we can't let our relationship distract from our jobs."

"Agreed, but we've done a good job so far of separating the personal from the professional," Rachel pointed out. "There's just more personal to keep separate now."

"Well, we need to get on a conference call, so let's put a pin in this until after work. Do you want to come home with me tonight?"

She gave me a big smile. "More than anything."

"Okay, Office Wife, it's a date."

Epilogue—Rachel

Four months later...

"I never thought I'd see my baby get married."

My mom pinched my cheeks between her fingers, smooshing my face together.

"Lay off her, Ma." My sister Sarah rolled her eyes over Mom's shoulder. "She's not a toddler. Besides, I'm the youngest, shouldn't I be your baby?"

"You're both my babies," Mom pacified her. She ran a critical eye over the dark pink party dress I wore. "I just wish you were wearing a wedding dress."

"It's a dress and I'm wearing it to a wedding," I pointed out. "By definition, that makes it a wedding dress."

"You know what I mean, young lady. And why couldn't you get married in a synagogue?"

She looked around the bedroom where we were getting ready. To our shock, when Madison Phoenix heard that Brittany and I were getting married, she offered to host us at her fancy house. We couldn't pass up that offer.

"Because we wanted something simple, Ma. Besides, you know Brittany isn't Jewish. I told you, she's Lutheran."

She sighed. "We could have at least brought in a rabbi to bless your union."

My response was interrupted by a knock at the door. It was my good friend and college roommate Margaret, who was serving as my maid of honor.

"It's show time. We'll see you down there, Mrs. Rosenthal."

My mother and sister left to find their seats, and Margaret made a show of checking out my outfit.

"You clean up nicely."

"Thanks."

Margaret had helped me pull my hair up into some kind of fancy updo, leaving tendrils of hair framing my face. With make-up on, I scarcely recognized myself.

"Are you ready to do this?" she asked, eyes studying my face.

"Yeah. I can't wait."

It was true. Brittany and I had decided to get married a couple of days after we started officially dating. Some people may have thought it was fast, but we had ten years of friendship to use as a base for our relationship. We didn't need to spend a lot of time dating to confirm what we already knew: we were perfect for each other.

"Okay," Margaret smiled. "Let's go get you wifed up."

Madison's house had a giant backyard and since the weather forecast was for a perfect summer day, we'd opted to get married outside.

We huddled in the kitchen until we heard music and then, by previous arrangement, Margaret walked down the makeshift aisle that had been created by placing a long red carpet on the grass leading up to a low stage Madison had set up for the ceremony. She was followed by Brittany's good friend, Colleen.

When they reached the stage, the wedding march started and Brittany and I each exited the house from different sides, meeting at the end of the aisle. My eyes widened in appreciation as I saw the ivory suit she wore, her blonde hair curled around her face.

"You look beautiful," I said, as I took her hand and we began walking up the aisle together.

We'd opted not to have any of our parents walk us up the aisle, much to my mother's consternation.

"So do you," she responded.

I was trying to be stoic, but Brittany was smiling widely, looking overjoyed at the idea of us getting married. Her joy was contagious, and I smiled alongside her as we reached Alice, the woman who was going to be performing the marriage ceremony. She worked at Phoenix Software with us, although she worked in the C suite with the other executives.

We'd been trying to figure out where to find an officiant on day while having coffee at Morning Jolt, and Madison's partner Camille overheard us and recommended Alice. It was the perfect suggestion.

We turned to face each other, standing hand in hand as we exchanged our wedding vows. Brittany and I had been living together since right after we'd gotten together romantically, but we were both excited to make it official in front of our friends and family.

I'd like to say that one of us did a romantic proposal, but the truth is, we were laying in bed pleasuring each other in a sixty-nine position when Brittany suddenly stopped and said, "We should get married."

"Sounds good, let's figure out a date," I'd responded before returning to one of my favorite activities: licking Brittany's pussy.

"I now pronounce you officially married," Alice said. "You may kiss."

I took Brittany into my arms and stopped with my lips an inch away from hers.

"I love you, Real Wife."

"I love you too."

Then we kissed and started our lives as a married couple just like we'd spent our time as friends: together.

***

Want to read about how Madison and Camille got together? Check out their story in *My Secret Crush*[1]. And you can read about Brittany's friend Colleen finding love with her high school nemesis in *My Valentine's Gift*[2].

You can find more of Reba's lesbian romances at
***Books2read.com/rl/lesbianromance*[3]**
If you liked this book, please consider leaving a review or rating to let me know.

---

1. *https://books2read.com/u/mVAR5r*

2. *https://books2read.com/MyValGift*

3. **https://books2read.com/rl/lesbianromance**

Be sure to join my newsletter for more great books. You'll receive a free book when you join my newsletter. Subscribers are the first to hear about all of my new releases and sales. Visit my mailing list sign-up at bit.ly/RebaBaleSapphic[4] to download your free book today.

---

4. https://bit.ly/RebaBaleSapphic

The Divorcee's First Time
A Contemporary Lesbian Romance
By Reba Bale

"It's done," I said triumphantly. "My divorce is final."

My best friend Susan paused in the process of sliding into the restaurant booth, her sharply manicured eyebrows raising almost to her hairline. "Dickhead finally signed the papers?" she asked, her tone hopeful.

I nodded as Susan settled into the seat across from me. "The judge signed off on it today. Apparently his barely legal girlfriend is knocked up, and she wants to get a ring on her finger before the big event." I explained with a touch of irony in my voice. "The child bride finally got it done for me."

Susan smiled and nodded. "Well congratulations and good riddance. Let's order some wine."

We were most of the way through our second bottle when the conversation turned back to my ex. "I wonder if Dickhead and his Child Bride will last for the long haul," Susan mused.

I shook my head and blew a chunk of hair away from my mouth.

"I doubt it," I told her. "Someday she's gonna roll over and think, there's got to be something better out there than a self-absorbed man child who doesn't know a clitoris from a doorknob."

Susan laughed, sputtering her wine. I eyed her across the table. Although she was ten years older than me, we had been best friends for the last five years. We worked together at the accounting firm. She had been my trainer when I first came there, fresh out of school with my degree. We bonded over work, but soon realized that we were kindred spirits.

Susan was rapidly approaching forty but could easily pass for my age. Her hair was black and shiny, hinting at her Puerto Rican heritage, with blunt bangs and blond highlights that she paid a fortune for. Her face was clear and unlined, with large brown eyes and cheek bones that could cut glass. She was an avid runner and worked hard to maintain a slim physique since the women in her family ran towards the chunkier side.

I was almost her complete opposite. Blonde curls to her straight dark hair, blue eyes instead of brown, curvy where she was lean, introverted to her extrovert.

But somehow, we clicked. We were closer than sisters. Honestly, I don't know how I would have gotten through the last year without her. She had been the first one I called when my marriage fell apart, and she had supported me throughout the whole process.

It had been a big shock when I came home early one day and found my husband getting a blow job in the middle of our living room. It had been even more shocking when I saw the fresh young face at the other end of that blow job.

"What the fuck are you doing?" I had screeched, startling them both out of their sex stupor. "You're getting blow jobs from children now?"

The girl had looked up from her knees with eyes glowing in righteous indignation. "I'm not a child, I'm nineteen," she had informed me proudly. "I'm glad you finally found out. I give him what you don't, and he loves me."

I looked into the familiar eyes of my husband and saw the panic and confusion there. I made it easy for him. "Get out," I told him firmly, my voice leaving no room for argument. "Take your teenage girlfriend and get the fuck out. We're getting a divorce. Expect to hear from my lawyer."

The condo was in my name. I had purchased it before we were married, and since I had never added his name to the deed, he had no rights to it. There was no question he would be the one leaving.

My husband just stared at me with his jaw hanging open like he couldn't believe it. "But Jennifer," he whined. "You don't understand. Let me explain."

"There's nothing to understand," I told him sadly. "This is a deal breaker for me, and you know that as well as I do. We are done."

The girl had taken his hand and smiled triumphantly. "Come on baby," she told him. "Zip up and let's get out of here. We can finally be together like we planned."

"Yeah baby," I had sneered. "I'll box up your stuff. It'll be in the hallway tomorrow. Pick it up by six o'clock or I'm trashing it all."

After they left my first call was to the locksmith, but my second call was to Susan.

That night was the last time I had seen my husband until we had met for the court-ordered pre-divorce mediation. He spent most of that session reiterating what he had told me in numerous voice mails, emails and sessions spent yelling on the other side of my front door. He loved me. He had made a terrible mistake. He wasn't going to sign the papers. We were meant to be together. Needless to say, mediation hadn't been very successful. Fortunately, I had been careful to keep our assets separate, as if I knew that someday I would be in this situation.

Through it all, Susan had been my rock. In the end I don't think I was even that sad about the divorce, I was really angrier with myself for staying in a relationship that wasn't fulfilling with a man I didn't love anymore.

"You need to get some quality sex." Susan drew my attention back to the present. "Bang him out of your system."

"I don't know," I answered slowly. "I think I need a hiatus."

"A hiatus from what?" Susan asked with a frown. "You haven't had sex in what, eighteen months?"

I nodded. "Yeah, but I just can't take a disappointing fumble right now. I would rather have nothing than another three-pump chump."

I shook my head and continued, "I'm going to stick with my battery-operated boyfriend, he never disappoints me."

Susan smiled. "That's because you know your way around your own vajayjay."

She motioned to the waiter to bring us a third bottle of wine.

"That's why I like to date women," she continued. "We already know our way around the equipment."

I nodded thoughtfully. "You make a good point."

Susan leaned forward. "We've never talked about this," she said earnestly. "Have you ever been with a woman?"

For more of the story, check out "The Divorcee's First Time" by Reba Bale, available for immediate download[1] today.

***

Want a free book? Join my newsletter and a special gift. I'll contact you a few times a month with story updates, new releases, and special sales. Visit bit.ly/RebaBaleSapphic[2] for more information.

---

1.   https://books2read.com/u/bpznKX

2. https://bit.ly/RebaBaleSapphic

Other Books by Reba Bale

Check out my other books, available on most major online retailers now. Go to my webpage[1] at bit.ly/AuthorRebaBale to learn more.

Friends to Lovers Lesbian Romance Series
    The Divorcee's First Time
    My BFF's Sister
    My Rockstar Assistant
    My College Crush
    My Fake Girlfriend
    My Secret Crush
    My Holiday Love
    My Valentine's Gift
    My Spring Fling
    My Forbidden Love
    My Office Wife
    My Second Chance
    Coming Out in Ten Dates
    Worth Waiting For

The Club Surrender Series
Jaded

Hated

Fated

Menage Romances
Pie Promises

Tornado Warning

Summer in Paradise

---

1. https://books2read.com/ap/nB2qJv/Reba-Bale

Life of the Mardi
Bases Loaded
Two For One Deal
The Unexpectedly Mine Series
Sinful Desires
Taken by Surprise
Just One Night
Forbidden Desires
Hotwife Erotic Romances
Hotwife in the Woods
Hotwife on the Beach
Hotwife Under the Tree
A Hotwife's Retreat
Hot Wife Happy Life

Want a free book? Just join my newsletter at bit.ly/RebaBaleSapphic[2]. *You'll be the first to hear about new releases, special sales, and free offers.*

About the Author

Reba Bale writes erotic romance, lesbian romance, menage romance, & the spicy stories you want to read on a cold winter's night. When Reba is not writing she is reading the same naughty stories she likes to write.

You can also follow Reba on Medium[3] for free stories, bonus epilogues and more. You can also hear all about new releases and special sales by joining Reba's newsletter mailing list.[4]

---

3.   https://medium.com/@authorrebabale

4.   https://bit.ly/rebabooks

Don't miss out!

Visit the website below and you can sign up to receive emails whenever Reba Bale publishes a new book. There's no charge and no obligation.

https://books2read.com/r/B-A-IDTM-FASLC

BOOKS 2 READ

Connecting independent readers to independent writers.

Did you love *My Office Wife*? Then you should read *My BFF's Sister*[5] by Reba Bale!

Her best friend's sister is strictly off-limits, especially when her friend has no idea that her little sister is a lesbian.

Jewel is back from a long stint in the Peace Corps and ready to start her new life back in her hometown. She's ready to come out to her family and live life without apology. A chance encounter with her sister's best friend Alice brings back memories of her childhood crush. Alice still sees her as the pesky kid sister, but Jewel is all grown up now and knows exactly how to take what she wants – and she wants Alice.

Can Jewel convince Alice to take a chance on love, even if it may destroy her longest friendship?

---

5. https://books2read.com/u/4NxD1J

6. https://books2read.com/u/4NxD1J

"My BFF's Sister" is book two in the "Friends to Lovers" romantic novella series. Each book in the series is a steamy standalone featuring an LGBTQ couple making the leap from friends to lovers. This book includes explicit sexual activity between consenting adults. It is intended for mature audiences only.

www.ingramcontent.com/pod-product-compliance
Lightning Source LLC
Chambersburg PA
CBHW022058150726
47990CB00003B/1149